For: Ewelina

Here's to all the balloons!
Soft Landings.
2021

soft
bright
fluffy

you and me

Special Shape balloons are typically larger in size, harder to fly, and require many more volunteers to crew than that of hot air balloons. Volunteering with a Special Shape crew is the perfect place to get involved and be a part of the ballooning community!

–N.A.

About the Author and Illustrator

Nancy Abruzzo is the author of *Pop Flop's Great Balloon Ride* (MNMP). She is a balloonist and the widow of Richard Abruzzo, world record holder of hot air and gas ballooning. Their two children are Mary Pat and Rico. Nancy is president of the Richard Abruzzo Foundation; past president and board of trustees member of the Anderson Abruzzo Albuquerque International Balloon Museum; and Albuquerque International Balloon Fiesta ambassador for international pilots team leader.

Noël Dora Chilton grew up in Albuquerque, hearing the roar of balloon burners overhead. She is illustrator of *Pop Flop's Great Balloon Ride* and other books. She lives in Hawaii with her two sons.

Director: Anna Gallegos
Editorial director: Lisa Pacheco
Art and production director: David Skolkin
Composition: Set in Chaloops
Manufactured in United States of America
10 9 8 7 6 5 4 3 2 1

Library of Congress control number: 2021935936
ISBN 978-0-89013-665-2 hardcover
ISBN 978-0-89013-666-9 ebook

Museum of New Mexico Press
PO Box 2087
Santa Fe, New Mexico 87504
mnmpress.org

soft
bright
fluffy

a fiesta of
special shape
balloons

written by
nancy abruzzo

illustrated by
noël dora
chilton

balloons go up
balloons come down
balloons fly

up

down

pigs
bees
penguin

you and me

witch
spiders
clowns

you and me

special you
special me
special shapes

up
down

frogs
elephants
owls

you and me

sun
tree
pumpkin

you and me

balloons go up
balloons come down
balloons fly

up
down

octopus
turtle
bears

you and me

dogs
cows
butterflies

you and me

special
you
special
me

special shapes

soft
bright
fluffy